JUST ME AND MY MOM

BY
MERCER MAYER

*For my new son Benjamin
and his Momma*

A Random House PICTUREBACK® Book

Random House 🏠 **New York**

Just Me and My Mom book, characters, text, and images © 1990 Mercer Mayer. LITTLE CRITTER, MERCER MAYER'S LITTLE CRITTER, and MERCER MAYER'S LITTLE CRITTER and Logo are registered trademarks of Orchard House Licensing Company. All rights reserved. Published in the United States by Random House Children's Books, a division of Random House, Inc., New York. Originally published in 1990 by Golden Books Publishing Company, Inc. PICTUREBACK, RANDOM HOUSE, and the Random House colophon are registered trademarks of Random House, Inc.
www.randomhouse.com/kids
Educators and librarians, for a variety of teaching tools, visit us at
www.randomhouse.com/teachers
Library of Congress Control Number: 89-82381
ISBN-13: 978-0-307-12584-2   ISBN-10: 0-307-12584-X
Printed in the United States of America
45 44 43 42 41 40 39
First Random House Edition 2006

We went to the city,
just me and my mom.
Mom gave me some money
to buy tickets for the train.

I wanted to help Mom get on the train
but the steps were too high.
So Mom helped me instead.

But when the conductor came by,
the tickets were gone.
So Mom paid the conductor
some more money.

The city was very busy.
I held Mom's hand so she
wouldn't be scared.

We went to the Museum
of Natural History.
They had rooms full of
old dinosaur bones.

I picked up a little dinosaur egg
to show to my mom.
But someone ran up and grabbed it.
I wasn't going to hurt it.

I tried on some costumes,
just for Mom.
But the museum guard
didn't like that.

DO NOT TOUCH

Then we went next door
to the Aquarium.

There were lots of fish
in a big tank of water.

They had some seals doing a show.
Mom got mad because
she couldn't find me.
I ran up front to get
a closer look at the seals.

PROGRAM

We went to the art museum,
but it only had a lot of weird pictures
and I was getting tired.

After that, we went to a very
nice restaurant for lunch.
We didn't stay, though.

We decided to have a hot dog from
a stand. That was more fun anyway.

Mom wanted to go to a big store
full of dresses and stuff like that. Yuck.

Mom even made me try on some clothes.
She bought me a new suit.
Some guy measured me and stuck pins all over
my clothes.

We passed by the toys.
I found the stuffed animal
I always wanted
but Mom said, "It's time to go."

We took a taxi to the train station.
I got to ride in the front seat.
The taxi driver drove real fast.
That was cool.

I let Mom buy the tickets this time.
She said she didn't have
enough money to buy more tickets
if these got lost.
"Good idea, Mom!"

We had fun, just me and my mom.
I even stayed awake
all the way home — well, almost.